This book is dedicated to S.S.

Paperback ISBN: 978-1-63731-985-7   Hardcover ISBN: 978-1-63731-986-4

Copyright © SEL Enterprise
Printed 2024 - All rights Reserved

We reserve all rights to copyright, illustrations, and design.

October was a **SPUNKY** girl,
With a magnifying glass in hand,
She'd crack a case in no time flat,
The **BEST** in all the land.

She loved to peek at calendars,
To see what each day would bring,
But one fine morning, to her shock,
Some important dates were **MISSING!**

She **HOLLERED** at her buddy Scarecrow,
"Hey, did you catch a clue?
My calendar's been swiped, it seems,
What am I gonna do?"

Mr. Scarecrow scratched his straw-filled head,
"The wind was **HOWLiN'** loud,
It tossed those pages left and right,
Like some crazy, restless crowd."

October gave a **PUZZLED** look,
"That wind was wild, no doubt,
But wind doesn't swipe your dates away—
Something's fishy here, no doubt."

She strolled over to the pumpkin patch,
Where Mrs. Pumpkin chilled,
"Any idea where my dates have gone?
This mystery's gettin' **REAL!**"

Mrs. Pumpkin **CHUCKLED**, "Well, I've heard,
'Bout some Holiday Hopper sneakin' by,
He skips through days like they're old news,
And loves to zip on by."

She set a trap with **SAVVY** skill,
Marked each date with a grin,
With pumpkins, witches, autumn leaves,
She knew just how to win.

She hid behind a pile of leaves,
And waited, heart a-thump,
The night was **COOL**, the stars were **BRIGHT**,
Her heart was set to jump.

The Hopper sighed and nodded fast,
"I just love holidays,
But I see now, I was **RUSHIN'** through,
And messin' up all your fun days!"

Now October's days are safe and sound,
Her days are **FULL** and **SWEET**,
She shares life with her pals around,
October's cool and can't be beat!

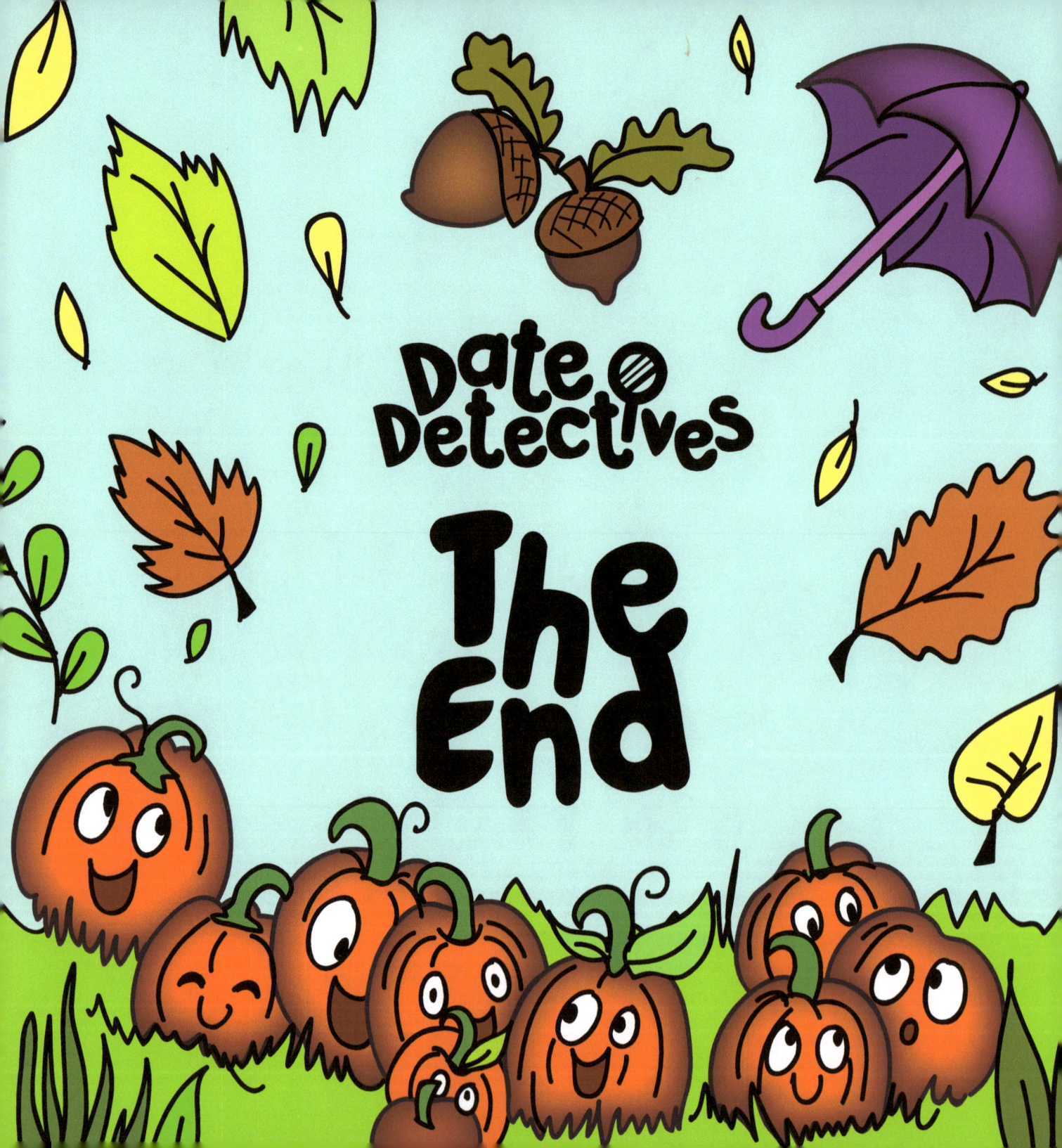

CRAFT ACTIVITY: LEAFY LANTERNS

Let's get crafty with a twist,
Make a lantern cool and bright,
It's simple, fun, and awesome too,
And gives a cozy light.

YOU'LL NEED:
* A CLEAR GLASS JAR,
* FALL LEAVES IN REDS AND GOLDS,
* SOME GLUE OR MOD PODGE, YOU KNOW,
* A BRUSH WITH GOOD, STRONG HOLDS.

INSTRUCTIONS:

1. GATHER LEAVES:

Go outside,
Scoop up some leaves with flair,
Clean 'em up, and get 'em ready,
For a craft beyond compare!

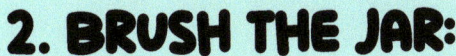

2. BRUSH THE JAR:

With Mod Podge first,
Stick the leaves with care,
Arrange them round the jar so neat,
For a lantern that's all square.

3. SEAL IT UP:

With Mod Podge on top,
Let it dry, then light,
Add a tea light to the jar,
And watch it glow so bright!

FALL RECIPE: PUMPKIN SPICE MUFFINS

Whip up a treat that's sweet and nice,
With pumpkin spice so rad,
These muffins are the bomb, you know,
The best you've ever had!

You'll need:
* A can of pumpkin, orange and bright,
* Two eggs, and sugar too,
* Some flour, spices, baking stuff,
* To make a treat for you!

Instructions:

1. Mix it up:

Crack those eggs,
Add sugar to the mix,
Toss in the pumpkin, oil too,
Stir it good—no tricks!

2. ADD THE DRY:

Toss flour in,
With baking soda and spice,
Pour it in the muffin tins,
They'll bake up oh so nice!

3. BAKE 'EM UP:

For twenty minutes,
In the oven hot,
Let them cool, then chow 'em down,
They're the best thing that you've got!

www.ingramcontent.com/pod-product-compliance
Lightning Source LLC
Chambersburg PA
CBHW041710160426
43209CB00018B/1793